Quiet Under a Violet Sky
A Cold Reality Told in 3 Volumes

By: Noah Jacobs
Cover Art: Gabe Pascua

To Charlie Brooker for his technophobia and Allen Ball for his complex interplay of characters.

More importantly, to everyone who helped me to bring some colors together into a portrait by taking the time to look at them with me before there was any coherence.

CONTENTS

PROLOGUE: THE HEAD OF MÍMIR

THE HEAD OF MÍMIR

Soon, a passing asteroid will make the moon turn purple.

The scientific explanation commonly shared by the media was that, due to a meteorite with significant mineral contents, Earth's magnetic field would be sent into disarray; this, when mixed with an expected burst of solar wind, would create a phenomenon similar to the Aurora Borealis. Of course, the science was far more nuanced than this, but no one had time for nuance.

The meteorite was popularly called the Head of Mímir, a title that lost its meaning on the vast number of people who used it in conversation, and understandably so. The individual who came up with the name was a Professor of Classicism, Gwen Southland. She worked at the same university as the astronomer who first learned about the event.

That particular astronomer's name was Peter Reinfield. At the time, Southland and Reinfield were lovers. So, immediately after Reinfield had made his discovery, he rushed over to Southland's office to tell her the news.

Although it was past 11 p.m., Reinfield knew that he would find Southland working in her office, restlessly searching for truth in old tomes or otherwise transcribing that truth in a new paper that only classicists, historians, and Reinfield would read. That was something painful to say, but Reinfield could say it--after all, *his* papers were generally only ever read by astronomers and Southland. This one, though, would be different.

When Reinfield got to her office, Southland was there, even though it was late. They both smiled, hugged. He was too aloof to realize that she was only still there in hopes that he would come visit her.

Reinfield explained what was going to happen. Southland understood it as much as someone who was not an astronomer could. This was because their relationship was composed of juvenile midnight trysts (much like what their students might engage in) and academic rants from the other's area of expertise.

As a result, Southland understood the concept enough to make the declaration that the otherworldly rock would be like the Head of Mímir.

"Say that again," asked Reinfield.

"Which part?"

"What'd you call the meteorite?"

"The Head of Mímir."

"What does it mean?"

Now it was Southland's turn to take Reinfield on a deep dive through the particulars of her own profession. Southland began explaining Norse mythology, telling of the decapitation of Mímir in the Æsir-Vanir War, followed by the acquisition of his head by Odin. Odin then carried Mímir around to receive counsel and wisdom whenever he needed it. Likewise, this rock that was detached from some celestial body far away in the cosmos would reveal wondrous secrets to the scientists who listened.

Reinfield couldn't agree more.

On their way out, Southland hit the lights and stood in the doorway to her office for a moment. She noticed how the streetlight slid in from the window behind her desk. It was a column of light that illuminated the books and essays scattered about.

The next day, when Reinfield hurriedly published a paper on the subject to much media attention, it was with the title, "The Head of Mímir: Why We will See a Purple Moon." The paper was prefaced with a brief summary of the significance of the title, as well as great thanks to Professor Gwen Southland for its conception.

Southland saw this in the copy that had been slipped under her door.

She smiled.

When the paper first came out, the media coverage often included the reasoning behind the naming as well as the scientific explanation of the phenomenon. Both Southland and Reinfield were happy.

However, as time went on, these details, important to both professors in different ways, were gradually omitted more and more. Of course, the scientists continued to speculate about the science, and the philosophers and poets mused on about what this meant for the human race; the public, though, quickly began to ignore the substance of the event. It was almost like they began to ignore the event itself.

Lists were circulated, touting knowledge of the "Ten Best Spots to Watch the Purple Moon" and "13 Ways to Prepare for the Head of Mímir;" shirts that said, "I Saw the Head of Mímir" were being sold; telescopes designed particularly for the event were being advertised. The term "Once in a blue moon" was commonly being replaced with "Once in a purple moon."

The event felt disgustingly commercialized to both academics. Reinfield was disappointed by how the public was ignoring all that the happening was going to give the scientific community, while there was a pang in Southland's stomach every time she saw an article reference the Head of Mímir; she knew that the term, once great in its rarity, was no longer being used with any weight. The very thing she thought to exalt had become commonplace.

It was by far the worst on the day the Moon was going to actually be turning purple. Somehow, it seemed as if no one was even thinking about it anymore. It was almost like the content about the event had become so saturated so quickly that it was now irrelevant. It was like seeing yourself in the mirror each day when you woke up--you stopped noticing you.

Perhaps the only solace for the two academics was that they would be able to watch the event together; Reinfield now had an army of eager young research assistants to collect all the data he would ever need from the event, so he had no reason to take the time to record any of it himself.

The pair used their access at the university to get on top of one of the taller buildings, the Museum of Natural History. Standing on the past, they would watch the future unfold above them.

As they waited, Southland and Reinfield discussed their joint frustration with the world. To *them* (a nebulous term meaning anyone who did not appreciate this event as they should), the miracle of the purple moon had gone from just another flashy piece of drama to a forgotten triumph before it had even occurred. It did not seem like *they* understood the true depth and power of the situation.

But how could the others understand? It was not their profession, not their job to know these things. Reinfield expressed hope that they at least comprehended the leaps and bounds that would be made by science, and not just as a surface level fact.

Southland mused on the difficulty of expressing with words the difference between merely seeing something and truly feeling it within one's soul. Why did it seem like everyone watched their own lives as if they themselves were just second rate TV characters, shallow and untrue?

The sun was setting; the sky was turning a brilliant red. Reinfield and Southand held one another's hand.

A shooting star glided across the sky--the Head of Mímir. Reinfield put his arm over Southland's shoulder. Behind the rock, there was a brilliant stream of purple.

Off in the distance, the sun was almost gone. The moon was becoming more visible, and it was revealing itself to be the darkest violet man had ever seen. Luminous. The world was washed in a deep, rich purple.

Southland and Reinfield embraced one another in their shared understanding of the sheer miraculous nature of such a moment.

In that tranquility, the Head of Mímir spoke to them both.

What did it matter if no one else heard anything?

After all, they were only human.

VOLUME I: DIFFERENT LIVES

NAIL BITING

"You killed my son, and you have to live with that."

The words rebounded inside the walls of Grace's head for days, weeks. But not months. Grace, like all people, often fell prey to the false conviction that a certain momentous event would be all that she would think of until death. The truth was that she would bury it just as the boy and his cold body were buried beneath the earth.

Then, one day, the rain would come down. And, since Grace had never reconciled with her decision, the sight it revealed would slowly kill her.

Grace bit her nails when she was nervous, but only when she didn't know that she was nervous. When she realized that she was nervous, she would commit to both stopping her nail biting and her nervousness. Since she could never really stop being nervous when she wanted to, the nail biting would resume within the next 3 minutes.

Friday was a day defined by this pattern for Grace. By some strange product of chance and fate and nature, or whatever it was that drove things to where they were supposed to be, she had ended up in front of a lever, holding a radio. Over the radio, a man had explained that the brakes on his trolley were cut and that he was unable to control the vehicle.

He had also explained the function of the lever that Grace was standing in front of: pulling it would switch the track the trolley was on, resulting in the killing of one man tied to the track rather than five.

The only way for the trolley to switch tracks would be for Grace to pull the lever--an action that would require Grace to have a great deal of confidence in her decision-making abilities.

So, she continued biting her nails.

In the large hall her entry level philosophy class was held in, Grace was sitting on the far right side of the fourth row. It was the third day of lecture, so students were largely uncommitted to a specific seat. Grace, however, had made the decision to sit in the same spot all three days--that way, if anyone was looking for her, they would know exactly where to find her.

And would you look at that: a cute boy sat down right next to her. Before long, she was biting her nails.

Grace had the choice of doing nothing. There was no one to catch what her face looked like. She could simply walk away from this absurd situation altogether, and coolly disappear into the mist of time. It was not her fault that these men were tied to a track, or that the brakes were cut on the trolley--how the hell did that even happen? All Grace had to do was refuse to play into this psychotic game. Just leave.

But she couldn't. That unconquerable feeling of guilt in her stomach convinced her once again of the great fallacy of mankind, that her potential decision would live with her forever. Even if she didn't pull the lever, she at least felt that she had to stay to make it clear that she didn't pull the lever because she felt like it was not morally permissible, not because she was disinterested enough in the situation to just walk away from it.

At the same time, though, what was the difference between not pulling the lever and walking away and not pulling the lever and staying? Both accomplished the same thing. Would she just stay to watch five men get mindlessly slaughtered by an unfeeling, unbreathing trolley? That was not something that she would want on her resume. But, then again, why would she put any of this on her resume?

"Philosophy is useful in that it gives you different frameworks with which you can determine whether actions are morally permissible or impermissible," began the professor. "Take the infamous Trolley Problem, for instance.

"What might you do if you were watching a trolley that had its brakes cut racing towards five men on a track, unable to move for one reason or another, and you were in front of a lever that would allow you to switch the track that the trolley was on, sparing the five, but taking the life of another man, similarly unable to move? Is it permissible for you to pull the lever?"

"Philosophy raises all sorts of incredible questions, such as why does this matter at all?" the cute boy muttered to Grace in the first of a series of feeble attempts to win her affection (after two or three of his statements, she stopped biting her nails when around him).

The cute boy did have a point in a way, though--when would Grace, or anyone for that matter, ever have to decide what to do in a case even remotely like the Trolley Problem?

Grace continued to bite her fingernails as she struggled to decide what to do in a case exactly like the Trolley Problem. She was lost. All she felt that she could do was wish she had paid more attention to what the professor had said.

What was the difference between pulling the lever and murdering a man? Was there any? And if there wasn't, was there a difference between not pulling the lever and mass murder? Since she was physically there, right in front of the lever, would she not be responsible for the life and death of these men either way?

"Now, a utilitarian would immediately say, 'Why, you have no choice but to pull the lever,'" the professor went on. "It is your duty to maximize the utility experienced by the collective human being, and the pleasure that the five men will find in existence if they do not die today will surely be greater than that found by the one man!

"That's fine and well, but what if you don't want to pull the lever? What if you feel that no matter what, willfully deciding to perform an action that resulted in the death of any person was murder? Why, then, Kant may be able to offer you some solution--according to him, you cannot pull the switch, it is absolutely impermissible! Intolerable! You'll be committing a crime against man!"

Grace could not describe how strongly she desired a clear answer to guide the decision she was about to make. What was the point of a Philosophy class if it couldn't even help her make a choice, a choice as seemingly abstract and frequently discussed as this one? Half of the philosophers that she learned about would tell her to do one thing, the other half would exclaim that she must do the complete opposite. Damned if I do, damned if I don't, mused Grace.

snip!

Fuck. Grace bit off more of the nail on her right thumb than she had intended. It was that weird, uncomfortable break that she would feel whenever she bumped her hand into anything. It would last for a few days. She hated that. Today was Thursday, so she would have to deal with it until Saturday, at least. Damnit. This is why she needed to stop biting her--

"You have 30 seconds to decide if you're going to switch the track. May God be with us all," spoke the voice over the radio.

30 seconds. Grace wasn't sure about the whole "god be with us all" part. She was enough of a nonbeliever that she preferred to not even capitalize the word "god."

25 seconds. She would have to decide soon, and all she could do was waste time getting distracted with trivial things. Her damn nail.

20 seconds. Down to business. Utilitarian or Kantian. Neither of them could ever be fully right. The truth had to be somewhere in the middle, it always was.

15 seconds. But there was no middle when it came to a binary decision. She either pulled the lever, or she didn't.

10 seconds. Was it murder if she walked away? It was already going to happen. Not her fault that everyone had ended up here.

5 seconds. But then was it murder if she switched the track? Five lives were at stake. Again, it's not like she set the situation up.

Grace pulled the lever.

The professor continued: "Philosophy never can give you an exact answer for anything. It acts as a ledger, a record of the debates of the years, the discourses of the centuries. It shows you how great men, and women, thought. It shows you what it means to think.

"I hope that is what you will take away from my lectures. I am not going to try to make you believe what I believe; I won't even tell you what I believe. But I will try to give you the tools to determine what you want to believe for yourself. Good Day. Class dismissed."

Grace knocked on the door of the mother of the man who she had redirected the trolley towards. That's how she was wording it now: redirected the trolley towards.

Grace felt that she owed an apology to this woman. After all, her son might be living, had Grace decided to walk away, or if she simply wasn't there at all.

Or if she didn't exist.

Grace was biting her fingers as she waited. The nail on her right thumb was still not fully regrown; it was only yesterday that she had bitten it off, only yesterday that she had redirected the trolley.

It was raining today. It was always raining on a day like today. Maybe that was why it was a day like today? No; even if it was the sunniest April day, Grace knew that today would still be a day like today. She knocked again and absentmindedly resumed biting her nails.

The door opened. Before Grace could say anything, the mother said, "You killed my son, and you have to live with that." The door closed back up before Grace could get out the apology she had recited a dozen times.

That night, Grace was restlessly rolling around in bed as the words rebounded in her head:

"You killed my son, and you have to live with that."

And live with that she did. But only that night, and the next, and the next, and the next, for about eighteen more nexts, eighteen more nights.

Each night, Grace felt a little bit less bad about the whole situation. Other things were happening. Her sister, Joyce, was about to turn 21. That could only be good for Grace. And Caitlin was getting with that quiet kid, Dylan. There was definitely some drama there. And that whole purple moon thing was supposed to happen soon, whatever that was. The condo development that she lived in would have a block party to celebrate it, that would be fun.

Enough was happening in Grace's life to throw dirt on the memory.

What's more, that very night, Grace rubbed the nail of her right thumb against her bedsheet and did not even register the sensation of discomfort that, a day ago, she had thought would be with her until the grave. That, too, healed quickly.

The mother didn't.

AN OPEN DOOR

Alastair thought back to when he was maybe 5 or 6, just beginning preschool or kindergarten. When his mother put him to bed, she would come to his room and sometimes read him a story.

When the story was finished, and she had successfully resisted Alastair's cries for another one, she would get up and go to the door. Before she left, she would ask: Do you want the door open, or closed?

Alastair would say that he wanted it open, each and every time. She would begin to close it but stop when just a crack of light was still coming through.

When Alastair was a few years younger, open had meant completely ajar. Over time, that sliver of light shrank and shrank. It was imperceptible on a day by day basis, but it was undeniable when charted out over years. Even though his parents thought that he was oblivious to this, Alastair took it as a slight, the first act of deception against him.

He would often dream about this door with the crack of light coming from it, as if it were in the process of opening. He was finally going to see what was behind it; he was somehow certain that it wasn't just his hallway on the other side. Right before it was revealed, Alastair would wake up.

Later, when he was maybe 9 or 10, Alastair dreamed that he was outside in his yard, playing catch with his father. They heard the howl of wolves as the beasts crept out from the woods around them.

His father told him to run inside, that he would stay and fight them to keep Alastair safe. So, Alastair ran from the danger.

He sprinted to his bedroom and hid beneath his sheets. Fear petrified him. He could not lift his head to view the rest of the room. Perhaps he was not strong enough.

Alastair never knew at what point he woke up from his nightmare. For the rest of his life, part of him would wonder if he was still in it.

Starting when he was 17 or so, Alastair experienced sleep paralysis. He would see things in the corner of his room, men made of shadows, who would run towards him, lunging forwards. Why did they want to kill him? He would always wake up the moment before the creature touched him.

Each time, he strained to move but could not. It was as if his body was contained in a cage that matched his form almost perfectly. It had only the slightest space between his flesh and its bars. Alastair felt like he was thrashing around, being shocked whenever he hit the sides of his skintight coffin, bouncing and flopping like a dying animal. Really, Alastair wasn't moving at all. He was locked in place.

Sometimes, it wouldn't be a shadow man in the corner. Sometimes, it would be his parents downstairs, his mom shouting that there was an intruder in the house. He wanted to get up, to grab something to defend her, but he could not. Still, he was frozen in place.

By the time he was 30 or so, Alastair rarely ever dreamed anymore.

TEARS IN RAIN

Roy awoke at 8 a.m. He put each one of his alarms on snooze, for the first time, the second, the third.

8:24 am. Roy got out of bed, already disappointed in himself. He did 63 pushups. He had started at 50, 16 days ago, increasing by one each morning. He had skipped a few times.

He went to the hall's bathroom and immersed himself in hot water. After, he looked at himself in the mirror as he brushed his teeth. He had a remarkable sort of silver hair. It was blond, really, but it always seemed to shine when it was hit by the light in the right way.

It was already 8:47. Class at 9:00 a.m. He finished brushing his teeth, then returned to his room to quickly throw the supplies into his backpack. 8:51, he was running down his dorm staircase. Got to his bike. Unlocked it. Checked the time. 8:52.

He weaved through the crowds and got to the building at 8:58, racked his bike. Knew he would walk in right on time, like usual, even though the plan always was to be 5 minutes early.

English. He had taken the college level course in high school and scored exceptionally on the placement exam; he even got credit through the university he was now attending. Still, it was required that he take it here as well.

10:30, he biked to the nearest dining hall. For lunch, he wanted to sit by someone new, as he promised himself he would do each day at the start of the year.

He gathered his meal and wandered to the seating area. He scanned the tables for someone who looked interesting. Everyone was with friends or sitting alone. He didn't want to intrude on either.

Roy sat by himself, as usual. This way, he would be able to collect his thoughts, decide what he was going to get done with the rest of his day.

He had class at noon. Econ. At 1:30, he would go back to his dorm, take a 20-minute nap, and then complete his English paper. Next, he would go to the gym and then eat dinner, get done at 5 or so. Then, he would get ahead in his Philosophy readings and study French for the rest of the night. With breaks, of course. Get to sleep early, 10 p.m., so that he could wake up at 6 a.m. and go to the gym before his 8:30 class the next morning.

As he ate, he kept looking up, hoping that someone he knew would round the corner, like Joyce.

Roy ate alone.

Roy went to Econ. He wanted to pay attention this time. 13 minutes in, he pulled his phone from his pocket and scrolled through Instagram. 20 minutes in, he put it down.

Roy looked at the girl ahead and to the right of him. Gorgeous. He would sit by her next time. During the last class, he supposed that he would sit by her this time. So, next time, for sure. He had to.

27 minutes in, his phone was back in his hand. Snapchat now. 39 minutes in, it was down. 45 minutes in, back to Instagram. The dance continued until the professor let the hall know that they were dismissed.

He took his bike back to his room. He sat on his phone until 1:57. He decided he could masturbate before his 20-minute nap, so he did. Went to sleep at 2:15. At 2:35, Roy snoozed his alarm. Then again at 2:39, and 2:43, and 2:47, and 2:51, and 2:55, and 2:59, and, for the last time, 3:03. His 20-minute nap was completed.

Roy went to the bathroom. When he returned, he proceeded to check his phone. At 3:21, he felt like he needed to start his English paper. As his computer loaded, he went onto his cellphone again. At 3:29, he finally started writing, after checking his email, of course. Tossed his phone on his bed, so he could really get going. He finished the first one and a half pages by 4:18.

Roy felt that he deserved a break, so he walked over to his bed and looked at his phone for 5 minutes. He brought it back to his desk with him. He continued the ritual he had started in Econ of up and down and up and down until 5:26, when he realized that he was hungry. He had not finished his English paper, but he had achieved the Herculean task of writing one more page.

[17]

Roy went to the dining hall closest to his dorm and looked at the gym on the way there. He decided to hold off on working out until the next morning. After all, he had barely gotten a start on his English paper and still had to study for French--some of the assignments for the class were due tomorrow. Like the gym, the philosophy readings would have to wait until the next day as well. They weren't due for a little while, anyways.

Roy passed a poster that advertised a school-hosted watch party for the impending purple moon. That would be cool, he thought.

Roy planned on eating a salad but settled for some fried fish and chips. Again, he sat by himself. After eating, he just sat in the cafeteria on his phone.

When Roy got back to his dorm at 7:26, he checked his cell phone again and caught up on all the messages that he missed on the walk between the dining hall and his dorm. 7:43, he needed to study French. He tossed his phone to the side and pursued the oh so highly exalted grade of A with an astonishing 49 minutes of concentrated effort.

Back to his phone.

It was now almost 9. If he wanted to go to sleep at 10, he would have to finish studying French and take a shower and brush his teeth first. It would be tight, so he sat on his phone for another 10 minutes before beginning the dance of French and iMessages that lasted him until 9:40.

Finally done, he got up and grabbed his toiletries. He went to the bathroom and stood under the hot water. Just stood. And masturbated. But mostly stood.

After completing his nightly rituals, he got back into his room at 10:19. He checked to see what he had missed on his phone. He still had to prepare his backpack for the next morning. So, he did. It took him until 10:33.

A second wind overtook him. Roy had told himself that he would finish his damned paper, so he would finish his damned paper. He retrieved his laptop and wrote until 11:03. He made it to a total of four and ⅓ pages. He felt accomplished, even though he would have to correct it tomorrow and find a few places to add fluff amounting to ⅔ of a page. No big deal. He was close enough to be satisfied.

Roy decided to reward himself with an episode of Family Guy and a hit from his dab pen. Last night, he had told himself he would not get high the next day just to prove to himself that he was not dependent. Now, it didn't matter what he was dependent on; he had accomplished a lot today.

After the third episode of the show, each one less than half-watched, seeing as he had paid more attention to his phone than the television, it was past midnight. Roy knew he had to go to sleep. So, he turned off his TV and went to the bathroom again. Then, he put his laptop away.

Got into bed.

Set the alarms on his phone.

Looked at it for 18 and ½ minutes.

Set it down.

Picked it up to look at it for another 7.

Set it down,

And, at 12:48, he went to sleep.

Roy did not notice the way the streetlight slid in through his dorm window from the world outside. It created a column of light that landed on the floor.

The next morning, Roy's first alarm rang at 6 a.m.

He did not wake until 7:53.

By then, Roy had missed the column.

This was nothing to hold against Roy; after all, he was only human.

ON VEGANISM

      Caitlin was on her first date with Dylan. The two had been friends for a while. She ordered first and picked a salad. He got a hamburger.

      Earlier, they had talked about the importance of the environment. Dylan said that he wanted to maybe be an engineer for an alternative energy company. How could someone who "cared about nature" stuff his face with a burger, the remains of an animal born for slaughter in a dreary factory farm in the middle of the country?

MICROWAVE

Numb.

The bracelet hung loose around his hand as he stood in the middle of his kitchen.

Numb.

That was the only way to describe it, really, the only way to describe what he had become.

The microwave dinged in the background, reminding him for the fourth time that yes, his perfect food was done. His perfect food in his perfect home on this perfect night. But was that enough?

There was a reason that he let the microwave ring for four rounds. He wanted to stand there, he wanted to feel time fleeing from his hands, he wanted to feel his life running from him as he was paralyzed. An insect among men.

Francis turned around and finally opened the door to the microwave. He pulled out the chicken and potatoes that had gone from once warm at their conception to cold at their refrigeration to warm at their microwaving and now back to cold in his hands. Again, he had been caught up in thoughts more pressing than reality, and the world did not wait for him.

Even this he could not do right, heat up his meal in the microwave without letting it grow inedible. That was alright, for he simply pressed the easy cook button again, another 30 seconds. As his dish rotated around and around behind him, three times, he looked at the stools in front of him.

Four of them set up against the bar blocking off his kitchen. It reminded him of the scene in that painting, that one painting, what was it? "Nighthawks," that was it. The cozy bar. Where it felt like the street had a roof over it, and there was a fire lit, somewhere on the inside, whatever that meant. What would that painting look like if it had a purple glow? Would it still feel as inviting?

The stools that were in his kitchen now, the stools with backs (chairs, he supposed), he watched how the light drifted through each of the three holes on each of their four backs.

Those three holes the manufacturer added for "style" were probably only there to reduce the amount of material that went into making them.

His daughters, Joyce and Grace, they never sat in those seats, not anymore. Nor did his wife. They never ate as a family. They just lived together.

Each blank space was a full one saved.

The buzzer went off behind Francis, for the third time since he had reset it. He removed his food from the microwave, leaving a blank space there, too.

ON CONSUMERISM

Dylan was on a date with Caitlin. He ordered a hamburger; she ordered a salad--she was vegan.

Even though Dylan did not think that being a vegan was a necessary sacrifice, he had no problem with the idea. To each her own.

However, he did have a problem with what this humanitarian type was wearing on her feet: Air Force 1's.

He had no issue with the shoe itself; he thought it looked fine, if not basic. It was the brand that produced the shoe that left a bad taste in his mouth.

Nike, brought to you by sweatshops in India.

How could Caitlin care about cows more than people?

WHAT GOES IN

"Will you go to the Christmas Dance with me?" Paul asked with all of the strength that his weak, chubby frame could muster.

Christine looked him up and down and simply said, "No, I can't."

"Why?"

"Because I want to go with someone else."

A few moments later, Paul messaged Christine's friend, Kelsey. He asked why Christine didn't want to go with him. Kelsey told him that Christine wanted him to stop following her around like a lost puppy.

At home later that night, Paul washed his hands, making sure that he purged them of all the soap by thoroughly rinsing them with water and then aggressively drying them with a towel. They could be wet, but he really didn't want to taste any soap.

Paul turned on his fan and opened the faucets to his shower and sink so that his parents or brother could not hear what he was to do. He closed the window shade and opened the toilet bowl. Next, he knelt down before it, an altar, and shoved his right hand in his mouth, making sure that it went all the way back and hit the fleshy part of his throat behind his uvula. He gagged.

It would only take three or four gags for Paul to see stuff come up. This number, of course, was in part dependent on how recently he had eaten and how much water was in his stomach. Another thing that factored in was that he was doing this so often--when he was just getting started, it might take closer to 10 gags before he saw anything leave his stomach.

When he finally did feel some of the food coming up, he quickly took his hand out of his mouth, letting the vomit and toilet water meet. Sometimes, his hand would not move fast enough to dodge the downpour, so he would have to decide on rinsing the waste off his fingers or plunging his still puke covered hand back into his mouth. It didn't really make much difference to him when he actually thought about it, since he was going to taste the vomit anyways.

As for how long Paul sat there, how much he expelled from his stomach, that depended greatly on his mood. Every once in a while, a few releases would be enough to clear his mind, to calm him, but, more often than not, he would have to keep going until he got close to the point at which he felt like he would not be able to give anything else from his stomach. This was one of those times.

Healthy? No. But Paul didn't care. On some days, he simply couldn't stand the feeling of anything in his stomach, the sensation of gravity weighing down on his gut, a bag of ugly cartilage resting in front of his spine, full of food and soda, all just sloshing around. On those days that it became all that he could think about, all that he thought others could think about, he had to take action. So, he did.

He did not feel that the process was inherently amoral in itself. However, he did wonder if he was conditioning himself to not be responsible for the consequences of his actions. Might it be better to leave the cake and cookies and fries in his stomach so that he could use the disgust he felt in the moment to prevent himself from over indulging ever again? He had tried that a number of times, and it had never worked. The momentary discomfort was always just that--momentary. So, he kept forcing himself to throw up.

In a few years' time, when Paul was a senior in high school, no longer a freshman, his bulimia had less of a hold on his life. He had started working out, gotten much more fit than he would have been had he simply continued throwing up. Every so often, he would return to his old ways, if only for a day.

And what of Christine? Did he still love her? He had never stopped, even if he was temporarily distracted by some other woman. He had been bitter at first, but a series of shared classes at a small school forced the two to become friends. Good friends. They joked about the past as Paul came into himself; he was still embarrassed about who he had been before, but that embarrassment lessened each time that he brought it out in the open. He never talked about bulimia, of course, but he would joke about his old lack of confidence, the fear he had once approached everything with.

Unfortunately for Paul, even though time could not kill his desire for Christine, time could kill Christine. It had beaten him in his race to her, just by running slightly faster than he ever could, as it always did to the hopeful. Christine died in a car crash when she was 17.

After the initial shock and horror of the situation subsided as much as was possible, Paul began to reflect on the uniqueness of this new position in which he found himself. Before Christine's death, Paul was the closest that he had ever been to being united with her. The two had finally gone to their Winter Formal together, and he had even kissed her at the end. Although it was not apparent that anything was to come of it, Paul was planning on using that situation to reach the mutual love that he had so often hoped for.

Now, Christine was dead. This left Paul with a desire that had sometimes festered and sometimes flourished over the course of four years. What was he to do with it?

BEFORE HE WAS A FATHER

Dylan watched the swimmers in the pool. Sometimes, he would stand in the sun to tan. Other times, when it was particularly hot, he would find it more bearable to sit beneath the canopy covering his chair. Or, depending on the position of the sun, he would sit in shade at the edge of the pool, legs in the water, head in the shadows.

He saw Joyce and Grace walking by to lay out and tan. He heard them talking about the moon turning purple soon. They smiled at him. He waved back. They knew each other, but not really.

He was hoping that he would be able to talk to them at the block party that was supposed to happen when the asteroid passed--he lived in the same community as they did, one of those idealistic condominium developments where everybody knew everybody. The epitome of middle America.

There were two young boys in the deep end, each around 9. Playing, splashing. Dylan had administered the mandatory test for them a few weeks ago; they had both passed. Since then, they swam in the deep end quite often.

An older pair of women, each maybe 60 or 70, got into the shallow end. They floated on foam noodles towards the rope that separated the deep end from the shallow end.

"Those boys are splashing, I don't know if we want to go over there," one said.

"I'm sure the lifeguard will move them for us if they become a problem," the other responded, loud enough for Dylan to hear.

Today, Dylan was standing. For some reason, he thought it was easier to ignore people when he was standing. Maybe it was because it made him seem like he was occupied with his job.

One of the women lifted the rope segregating the two sides of the pool, and they both ducked under it.

Dylan watched the young boys. One of them appeared to be moving in such a way that his splashes got closer and closer to the path that the women were taking. He must have heard their earlier comment, too.

The boy did this in the way that you think is clever when you are around 9 years of age. He hoped that his subterfuge would go unnoticed by the soon to be soaked women.

The more vocal of the women caught the ambush that was being prepared. She said, "Lifeguard, these boys are getting awfully close to splashing us."

This pool was the kind of place where Dylan and the other employees were frequently gossiped about and put under scrutiny for the smallest of errors. It was also the kind of place where he knew that he would be brought up as the week's bit of drama at the next board meeting if he failed to placate the geriatric elitism welling up inside of the woman.

Dylan walked over to the boys and beckoned to them by lightly blowing his whistle in the way that said *I need your attention* rather than *you're in trouble.*

Dylan reviewed the options in his head one more time. He preferred not to tell them just to stay away from the women; that would certainly be nothing more than a minor band aid for the tensions. It would result in an escalating conflict far worse than the Cold War had been.

"If you two want to splash, you're going to have to do it in the shallow end. You can be in the deep end, but I don't want you accidently hitting anybody."

The woman who cared more was smiling triumphantly, trying to make eye contact with Dylan so that the pair could revel in what she perceived to be their shared victory. Dylan saw her eyes through his aviators but made no move to recognize them. Instead, he glanced at Joyce and Grace.

Neither were paying attention.

The boys were very upset, especially the one who had been intending on splashing the women. The boy simply looked at his friend and said, "Come on, let's get out. This isn't fair, the shallow end is no fun. We'll come back when they leave."

The boys found their parents and presumably had lunch at the club house. An hour after they had gone, they were back. The women were still in the pool, and Joyce and Grace were still laying out in the sun.

The boy who was more vocal walked over to Dylan and asked him if they could splash in the deep end yet.

"Not until those two leave," Dylan responded.

"How is that fair? *We* were here first," the boy argued, making a motion to include his friend who was nervously standing a few feet back.

Dylan didn't think it was fair either, so he lied. "When you're *older*, you get more privileges," he said, with emphasis on the word older.

The boy had the start of tears in his eyes at this point, the pure rage and frustration of a child just now understanding how unfair the world is.

"Well, some people abuse those privileges," the boy said through a shaky voice. He then jumped into the pool.

He began to swim back and forth underwater, making eye contact with no one, only coming up for air. This lasted for about 20 minutes before his parents told him it was time to go. His friend had already dried off; he hadn't even bothered to get back into the water.

After the boy had his clothes on and was walking away, both the women got out of the water. The loud one waved at the boy and said bye, making sure that he noticed her exit from the pool.

Dylan looked at Joyce and Grace. They were still not paying attention.

After the old women dried off and left, a feeling of relief washed over Dylan. Finally, there were no more children in the pool.

A CLOSED DOOR

Alastair was laying alone in a bed in a hotel. He slept on his back. Part of him hoped that this would bring back the sleep paralysis that he experienced when he was younger.

That way, he would at least come to feel something.

His wife of nearly 20 years was lying in another bed, one that he was supposed to share with her. She had upset him tonight, so he had driven off. He knew that this would make her cry.

When he had been younger, Alastair had convinced himself that he would never get married. Too much commitment. Now, even though he was wearing a wedding ring, he still thought this last part to be true.

Perhaps the only thing that had held him to her was their son, Peter. He was older now, about to graduate, right? Maybe it was time.

He wondered if Peter would be crying if he knew that his mother was alone?

Alastair did not think so. Peter was Alastair's son, and Alastair did not cry.

Alastair did not believe anything could make him cry, not anymore.

SUMMER DAYDREAMS

Peter went for a walk through his community on the kind of hot, summer day on which the breeze created by moving was relieving enough that you didn't want to stand still.

Peter lived in one of the countless cookie cutter developments that were all hastily constructed as promises of easy riches just before the housing crisis revealed itself. There were no sidewalks, but the light gray street had grass shoulders all the way around. If you wanted to, you could even walk pretty far into the road; no car would ever go fast enough to hit you.

On Peter's left, he was passing Joyce and Grace's house. The sisters were stretched out across their roof, side by side, both tanning. He noticed their long, bronzed bodies in bikinis. He saw that Joyce had her ass up, while Grace's breasts were exposed. Peter stared at the two as he walked by.

He then saw the development's pond to his right, a great big spot of blue. Not large enough to warrant the ownership of much more than a couple of paddle boats and kayaks by the association, but large enough for ducks and fish to call home.

Peter wanted to walk over to the dock that jutted into the water. People used it to fish. Peter wanted to use it to jump into the pond and cool off. But people never swam in those kinds of ponds, so Peter kept walking down the gray street.

When he was back in his house, Peter sat in a low beanbag chair that he kept towards the corner of one wall of his room. From there, he could see his large window that led onto his roof. In front of half of the window was a desk with a chair. He would open the other half of the window to get out onto the shingles when he wanted to. He imagined that this room was similar to the one that Joyce and Grace used to get onto their roof. He wondered whose room it was in their house.

In the early morning, the rising sun would slide in through the window and create a column of light that landed by the headrest of his bed. Peter wondered if Joyce or Grace ever noticed something like that.

The beanbag chair was low enough and the window was high enough so that when he was seated, Peter could only see the sky rather than the street below. The effect created quite a peaceful environment; when he was looking at the window from the beanbag chair, he could be wherever he wanted.

Sometimes, he would pretend that he was sailing away on a boat, or in some sort of flying ship. Sometimes, he would be in a home in a vast, open prairie, deep in the middle of the country. Other times, he would be in a villa in Europe. It didn't matter. He could be anywhere that he wanted. After hearing about the Head of Mímir, he even pretended that the sky was purple every once in a while.

But, on this particularly hot summer day, Peter pretended that he was in Joyce and Grace's house. He pictured Joyce appearing in the window, opening it. She then slid into the room, followed by her sister.

Peter was feeling himself now.

It was the kind of hot, summer day on which the breeze created by moving was relieving enough that you didn't want to stand still.

VOLUME II: COME TOGETHER

FAMILY TIME

It had been a month or so since Grace had redirected the trolley. She was sitting in the family's den with her sister. Their mother was nowhere to be seen.

"Hear about Dylan and Caitlin?" asked Grace.

"They're like four years younger than me, why should I care?"

"I don't know, I just thought you might find it interesting."

Joyce was on her phone. Grace was biting her nails.

Francis walked in. It was 4:30 p.m.

"Hey girls, good day?" he asked.

"Don't you have a job?" asked Joyce.

"I got out early to spend time with my family," Francis said defensively. He continued, "Where's Mom?"

"We don't know," said Grace.

"She's *your* wife," said Joyce. She looked up from her phone for this one.

"I wanted to have a family dinner at about 5 tonight. I told her that."

"Sounds like she doesn't care," said Joyce.

Grace looked at her father and said, "I made plans with some friends tonight, dad. I'm sorry. Just trying to take my mind off of things, you know?"

"I understand, Grace. Do what you need to." He was being sincere. "What about you, Joyce? Dinner with the old man?"

"I'm talking to Rachel. We're gonna hang out soon. Besides, I shouldn't have to if Grace doesn't."

Francis sighed.

"Well, what are you guys doing when the moon turns purple? You're going to the block party, right? What about after that? Do you want to watch the sky together, like old times?"

"I already have plans after," said Joyce. "I'll be 21 by then, remember?"

"What about you, Grace?"

Grace wanted to say yes, but she also hoped that she would find someone to spend the night with; she hadn't had something special in a long time. "I might be free, Dad. I'll let you know." She smiled at him. He smiled back. Joyce got up, typing on her phone as she did. She left without saying goodbye.

Francis went upstairs.

Grace continued to bite her nails.

GUILT, OR A STRIP CLUB

Alastair took a long pull from his cigar, hoping that the steadily increasing buzz would drown out that ever-present pang of guilt in his stomach. There was a stripper's ass right in front of his face.

It really was a terrible thing. Guilt, not the ass. It was ironic that Alastair thought he could deal with it by coming to a place like this. He got up with his half-consumed Death in the Afternoon and half-smoked cigar and sat as far away from the stage as he could while still seeing it. He felt bad being that close to the strippers and not tipping them. That was one thing he could feel bad about.

The problem would sometimes get worse when he moved, though. At that point, some of the girls would identify him as wanting to feel in control, even at a place like this. They would try to give him the illusion of power, a couple of them gravitating to the chairs surrounding him, starting up a conversation. They would tell him about their lives in hopes that when it was their turn on stage, he would feel an identification with their suffering that would lead him to open his wallet.

The girls would do this to Alastair at whatever strip club he went to. Sometimes, it would work on him. Sometimes, it would not.

Either way, when he handed them money, he understood why.

Sometimes, when he wouldn't budge, one of them would get a little flustered: why was he there if he wasn't tipping? Judging by his outfit, he clearly had money. And it wasn't the flashy, showy kind of getup either. It was the subtle, elegant, I-would-be-this-sleek-even-if-I-was-broke kind of look. But everyone who had that look knew that it wasn't true. That's why you never saw a broke guy looking like that.

Alastair didn't come here for the strippers, though. Or the alcohol or smoking, although it was all nice. He primarily came here to take his mind off of the idea that he was a bad person. Here, he could look around at all the hypnotized eyes and watering mouths, and he could tell himself that any sin which he committed was a product of his base instinct. Here, he was not responsible for any harm he had done to another.

He always knew that it really was his fault, though. Deep down, he understood that every time that he had been selfish, every time he had glorified wealth and pleasure, every time he smirked at what he thought was an unintelligent remark, or snapped at a friend, every time he had cheated in high school and college, or lied to a coworker or his boss, every time that he had blamed his dishonesty on a broken system that deserved to be gamed, every time he had given his wife the cold shoulder, every time he had disappeared on her, every time he had ignored his father, every time he had ignored Peter, every time he had shouted at his family or even screamed at them, every time he had not held his wife when he knew that she had been afraid, every time that he had made her afraid, on purpose, every time he had kept going when he knew that she wanted him to stop, every time that he had slept with a woman who wasn't her, every time he had wished another dead, every time he had thought about killing them, vividly and in crisp detail, every time he had thought about ending all of them, every time, it was all his fault. Deep down, he knew it.

But, with a cigar in one hand, a drink in another, and the knowledge that every man in the room was thinking about sex and every woman was thinking about money, Alastair felt better. Every time.

After all, he was only human.

GRAVEYARD

Roy stumbled through a graveyard. He took a swig of the fifth of whiskey in his hand and sat down in front of a tombstone. There was a light fog on the ground. His remarkable silver hair shined under the light of the lamps dotting the place.

He looked around him. Of all of the hundreds of bodies here, there was not one who he met when they were alive.

The tomb in front of him bore the name of Christine. He had never known a Christine. There were two different years written down with a dash in between them.

Roy had once read a poem about that dash being all that mattered. Roy took another pull from his drink.

Christine's dash was small. 17 years. Roy's own dash would already have more time to it, 19 years.

Roy stood up, began wandering again, continuing to drink. He wondered how much more eerie the place would be with a purple moon?

Just outside the fence of the graveyard, there was a sidewalk. Other students walked up and down it to get to some of the frat parties up the street. Roy saw them, groups of 2, 3, or 4, sometimes 5, laughing and joking and drinking under the stars.

What was today, Friday? Yes, tomorrow would be Saturday. Tomorrow, Roy would join the others. He would laugh and joke and drink under the stars, with them. Tomorrow.

Roy saw a large obelisk. There was a mist at its base. He walked over to it and read its inscription. The words were very specific to the person who had died. He did not know who the person was or who they had been. Roy continued searching.

A crow cawed above him. No, it was dozens of crows, as numerous as the gravestones. They were scattered about the black, gaingly trees. A murder of crows. Roy never understood why they were called that, a murder.

Roy tripped over one of the rocks lining the path, stumbling into the mud. He looked up and peered through the fog to see a mausoleum 30 feet ahead of him. He had not realized that he had been walking towards it. He picked himself up and proceeded to the menacing mouth. He climbed the steps and tried the door. It opened.

Inside, the walls were lined with large squares. Roy was sure that behind each of them was a coffin. A corpse.

Maybe ashes.

The building itself was shaped like a cross. In the center, there was a sarcophagus made of marble. Its sides rose to a perfect point in the middle, an infinitely small line that ran almost the length of the whole thing. A pyramid.

Through a little window at the back of the mausoleum, light from the lamps outside slid in. The beam ran through the thick, dusty air so that it seemed to make a shining column that had volume and landed on the sarcophagus.

Roy touched the pyramid where the ray hit.

He thought about the skeleton inside the stone prison. It was unable to see the ray of light. The coffin was in the way. Roy took another drink of his whiskey and then poured some on top of the sarcophagus; he thought that if he were dead and could not see something so quiet and beautiful, he would at least want a drink. The skeleton might, too.

Roy heard the crows continuing their incessant shrieking outside.

They sound like death, he thought.

A murder of crows.

Roy felt the bottle in his hand; he had emptied a little over half of it. He took one more long swig and then left the rest in the mausoleum for the others.

He exited the tomb and began heading towards the graveyard's open gate.

On his way out, he saw an obelisk, exactly the same as the one he'd seen earlier. But it was for a different body.

Out of curiosity, he walked over to it and read the inscription. Even though it was identical to the monument he had already observed, it had words describing a different person. A different life.

Roy looked up at the crows. Again, they shrieked a horrible shriek.

Drunk, Roy left the graveyard and wandered back to his dorm. He passed party goers the whole way.

He was sure that the crows watched him the entire time.

PASSIONFRUIT

Joyce had always believed that if she were to eat seeds, then fruit would grow inside of her stomach. This belief was perfectly understandable for a young child to have, seeing that the seeds of cherries were routinely spit out rather than swallowed, that apple cores were done away with, and that blueberry seeds were altogether too small to be perceptible.

At the time that Joyce was 7, she had run into no information that would serve to shake her belief system. Moreover, if she were to tell an adult about her deeply held principles, of course they would find it amusing and humor her; after all, when it was useful, adults could treat children like they didn't have the capacity to develop an understanding of the world. As a result, trivial things such as Joyce's belief that the seeds of fruit would grow in her stomach went unchecked during the first days of her youth.

It was by some absurd combination of chance and oversight, though, that Joyce's ideas went unchallenged all the way until she was 21. No one had ever explicitly told Joyce that her belief was, in fact, wrong. Until she was 10, the ideas were still viewed as the musings of a child. Until she was 13, it was thought that her holding this belief was the product of the will of a girl to extend the golden days of her youth indefinitely. Beyond the age of 14, everyone began to think she was just joking; they mistook her seriousness on the subject for a poignant brand of sarcasm.

On her 21st birthday, Joyce was at a bar. Many of her friends were buying her drinks. One of her friends in particular, John, liked to think of himself as part of the "in" crowd, more knowledgeable than the rest of the party about what was "hip." John ordered Joyce a passionfruit & ginger cocktail, a relatively obscure beverage that was oftentimes served with the actual seeds of a passionfruit.

When Joyce saw the seeds floating in the cup that John had gotten for her, she was already 3 or 4 or maybe 6 drinks in. She asked John what the hell seeds had to do with alcohol, to which John promptly and pompously replied, "What! You've never heard of a passionfruit & ginger cocktail? It's absolutely to die for. I'll drink it if you don't."

"What about the seeds? They'll grow in my stomach!"

"At least try it, Joyce."

Despite the breach of belief that it required, Joyce steeled herself and downed the beverage. One time wouldn't hurt.

The seeds couldn't grow *that* fast, right?

SELFISH

"Are you sure a divorce makes sense, Alastair?" asked Francis.

"She has nothing for me anymore. I can't force myself to love her. I feel like I'm cheating by staying with her."

The pair was sitting in two of the four chairs at the island in Francis's kitchen. They were drinking together. Grace was listening from the other room, biting her nails.

"What about Peter? How do you think he'll take it?" Francis inquired.

Alastair stared at the whiskey sour in his hand, thought for a moment. Then, he spoke: "I think he's old enough. He's quiet and strong. And he'll be off at college soon. This year actually, I think. Is he in the same grade as your kids?"

"Joyce's been in college for a couple years, and Grace is a freshman at the same place."

As if on cue, Joyce walked in through the door coming from outside and attached to the kitchen, drunk.

"Happy 21st, honey," said Francis. "How'd you get home?"

"John dropped me off."

"Good, I'm glad you didn't drive."

"Looks like you could use another drink," joked Alastair.

"You're Peter's father, right?"

"Yes, I am."

"No wonder Peter's getting so attractive."

Francis cringed. In the other room, Grace did, too. Alastair gently grinned.

"I'm sorry, Alastair, I think Joyce had a little bit more than she should have."

"We all do on our 21st. Should we help her upstairs?"

At that, Grace came in from the next room.

"Hey, Joyce. I'm glad you got home safe." she said.

"Fuck you," slurred Joyce. The words had a joking undertone and a hint of camaraderie, but they still stung.

[43]

"Come on, let's get upstairs" prompted Grace.

"Thanks, Grace," Francis said. "Again, sorry, Alastair."

"No worries, none at all," said Alastair. And then, as Grace and Joyce walked out, "See you girls at the block party."

A moment of silence.

"Did you get hit by something, Francis?"

Francis had what looked like a bruise on the bridge of his nose. It was fairly obvious, but it was the first time that Alastair said anything about it.

"No, I think it was a bug bite. It keeps getting worse."

"If it's not down by the party, these assholes won't give you the end of it. 'What happened to Francis's face? Was he in a fight?'"

"If I hear that shit, it will turn into a self-fulfilling prophecy. I think you're maybe the only person who hates them all more than I do."

"I don't hate them, Francis. I just actively dislike them."

Francis laughed.

"I'm going to tell her tomorrow, Francis."

"You both just seem so content."

"I think that she is. I'm not. This way, though, we both will be happy. And free."

"What will you do afterwards?"

"Maybe I'll sail the world."

At that, Alastair downed his drink. Fancis did the same.

ELEVATION

Grace sat on Joyce's bed with her.

"You okay, Joyce?"

"I'm a little worried."

"About what?"

"I drank something with seeds in it tonight." Grace took this sentence as Joyce's way of saying her stomach was upset.

"Do you think you're going to throw up?"

"Yes. I've never felt this bad before."

Grace helped Joyce to her bathroom. Joyce was afraid. She knew that if she did not puke now, it might be too late in the morning. The seeds may already have taken hold at that point. Now was her only chance.

Grace held Joyce's hair as she emptied her stomach. It was easy for Grace to forget about the trolley, most of the time. For some reason, she focused on it when she had no one to talk with about it.

Joyce's vomit filled the toilet.

An altar.

CLEAN

That night, Francis was sitting in his bathroom, alone. His wife was out, who knew where.

For the first time, he saw the grime in his bathtub. The unit was built into the wall, a porcelain cove. He had been meaning to clean it for the longest time. He remembered his mom, so long ago, telling him that he should make a weekly habit of it--perhaps he should have listened.

Now, he dragged his finger against the plastic walls. It was the womb he had stood within after so many stressful days, letting the hot water wash over him. And now, he found that a streak of white was appearing behind his finger. This was a new, pure white, slightly different than the old yellow one that he had gotten so used to. Francis liked this new color, he liked it a lot more than the old one.

He was hearing all of the past yell at him at once: "You've been one lazy son of a bitch, haven't you? All your life, actually? What have you ever gotten done? Well, I frankly don't give a fuck, because your bathtub is a mess, and your life is, too." It all spoke at Francis like that with fury, all of this grime, the composite of years of passivity.

If he had missed this thin film of dirt for so long, what else had he neglected?

Where was his wife?

Francis looked at himself in the mirror, and he saw a different man than the one who once had a clean bathtub and ambition just as clear. There was that bump on his forehead from something early that day. It was right at the bridge of his nose, but a little off to one side, so that his left eye well had become swollen.

It was really quite amazing how different it made him look to himself. Francis was taken by how calibrated his brain must have become to the image of his own face, seen like that, every day in the mirror. Of hundreds of thousands of data points, this was the one event that could throw it all off, throw the rest of them out the window.

Francis's face had looked different throughout his life, gradually changing, day by day. His brain understood this. It had charted a course, what Francis's face would look like tomorrow, what Francis's face would look like in two tomorrows, what Francis's face would look like in three tomorrows, so on and so forth to infinity. Francis knew that he would grow old, but that was easily accounted for when you took the change little by little. It would make sense.

This swelling, though, was something that his brain could not reconcile with itself. Therefore, it had to reject it by forcing Francis, every time that he caught a glance of his distorted face in the mirror, to do a double take. He would catch his own reflection out of the corner of his eye, and his neck would snap so that he could get a better look at this new feature.

His face and his bathtub.

Francis breathed. He knew that the swelling would go down. As for the grime, he would clean that tomorrow. Right now, he had just drawn a bath full of hot water, so he slid in between two, off-white walls.

And he knew that Alastair was going to be free.

MUST COME OUT

Five years after Christine died, Paul won one of the coveted seats as an Associate Consultant at a major firm he and his college classmates had all fought over. He was on a path to success that few could deny.

One night, he went to a club, the very exclusive kind that he was only able to enter with the help of a Principal at his firm; the Principal had taken a liking to Paul, so the pair went here to celebrate the closing of the first case that he was on.

Paul ended up taking a girl home. Her name was Christine. Had Paul seen her sober, he would have recognized her as bearing a decent resemblance to the Christine who he had once known; seeing her as he did now, under the influence of a large quantity of drugs and alcohol, Paul recognized her as the actual Christine he had once known.

He was sober enough to not bring this up at the club. Once the two were alone in his impressive apartment, however, he explained to her just how much he missed her. This Christine was a little confused, but continued to go along with it, as her mental state was no less foggy than his.

As their contact escalated, so too did Paul's reminiscing. As he brought up specific memories, Christine began to understand that she was being confused for someone else and was becoming clearly frustrated, a little uncomfortable even.

As Paul began to explain himself, she did not take kindly to his wondering why she had come back into existence, so she got up and began to leave. Paul desperately followed behind, going as far as to trail her to the elevator.

"Jesus Christ, what the fuck are you on? Stop following me like a lost puppy." The elevator closed as the words left her mouth.

If Paul was not fully convinced of her identity before, he was now.

Paul loved Christine. And now he had another chance to make himself better for her. So, he would. He went back into his apartment, kneeling down before his toilet.

An altar.

HOPE AS A HAND

"You have a pretty heartbeat," murmurs Dylan. He looks up at Caitlin, and she smiles. This was perhaps the best moment that he would spend with her.

Caitlin begins to tell Dylan a story, a story about another boy named Peter.

In the past, but not anymore, Caitlin had one of those weird, could've-been high school romances with Peter. They never dated or anything, but they liked each other on and off, especially when the other was taken. It just never timed out properly.

Caitlin wasn't worried about this; she knew that Dylan wouldn't care. What she felt guilty about, even though she truly had no reason to, was something Peter had done more recently, while Caitlin had been with Dylan.

"When I was in Chicago with our Marketing Club, one night Peter and I were talking, alone, at the restaurant in the hotel that we were staying at. Most everyone else was out a couple blocks down at another restaurant, but I had stayed back. Peter had, too, partly because of me, I'm sure."

"Did he ask you to fuck?" Dylan chided.

"Well, I'm getting to that," Caitlin said. "We were just talking about everything, how it never worked out between us. How it almost did so many times. You know? Just sorting out the past, kind of."

Dylan nodded.

"Then he told me that if I wanted, I could go back to his room with him."

"To fuck?"

"No, so we could stare at each other's naked bodies five feet apart. Yes, he wanted to fuck me. I didn't do it, of course, but... it's weird, you know? I feel guilty about it, even though I rejected it. I felt guilt about being offered something that I know I would never take."

This was not the first time that Caitlin had brought Peter up. It truly didn't bother Dylan, though, not in the way that

[50]

Caitlin was afraid it did. Dylan wanted more than anything for Caitlin to be happy, and if that meant that 2 or 3 or 4 years from now, she would be married to Peter, then that was honestly what Dylan wanted.

Three months before he had met Caitlin, a foreigner had come to town, so to speak; an exchange student from Spain began her year at Dylan's high school. Her name was Maria.

She was unrestrained by the somehow comparative modesty of the native students, and, for this, they hated her. Dylan was her only friend. Not only did he respect her for her freedom, but he wanted her for it, too.

Unfortunately, Maria had made it painfully clear that she did not want him. Not quite in a cruel way; it was more pitiful, really, a mercy killing. Dylan had rationalized it being a product of the fact that he was so close to her as a friend that she didn't want to jeopardize that.

This played in as a factor, perhaps as much as a fancy seeming glass plays as a factor in making whiskey taste more expensive and justifiable. Regardless of the glass, it would still numb your mind and purchase your silence with some cheap euphoria, all so that you could not feel it slowly poisoning your liver.

Maria would tell Dylan about the guys she fucked quite regularly. She actually fell in romantically with one of Dylan's best friends. This was its own kind of pain. At times, Dylan succeeded in overcoming the urge to think about it, but, at others, the sight of them was like death to his fragile delusions.

One of the reasons that she told him that she would not date him at the start of it all was that she did not want to date *anyone* during her time in America--she wanted to be free, like the eagle which the nation is so proud of.

Well, she was free; free to date Dylan's friends.

"It really doesn't bother you, does it, Dylan?" prodded Caitlin.

"I said I'd beat his ass, didn't I?"

"You didn't mean it, though, you still don't mean it."

"Of course, I do."

"No, you don't."

"I just want you to be happy, Caitlin, and if that means getting with Peter, then by all means, go for it."

[51]

She hit him on the chest. "That's not at all what I said, Dylan. Are you even listening?"

One night, Dylan was very drunk and at a party. He was just beginning to see Caitlin, but the two had not committed to anything. She was not there.

Maria was, though, and she was still dating Dylan's friend. Everyone knew that it wouldn't last much longer; it would probably end before the next weekend.

It had become quite apparent that Maria was into more than just guys at this point, and as much as this might raise her sexual stock with most men, it made Dylan's friend uncomfortable. The problem was not at all in the fact that she was also attracted to other women, but in the fact that she acted as if this gave her license to flirt with them in front of her boyfriend. The effect this had on him was the opposite of what she anticipated; rather than making him more into her, it made him uncomfortable and uncertain about the direction of their relationship.

So Dylan was not quite surprised when he stumbled into a room to see Maria making out with another girl on a couch--strangely enough, it was one of the girls that Dylan's friend had been worried about. Funny how these things happen.

Dylan *was* quite surprised, though, when Maria stopped making out with the girl and held out her hand to grab his. He was more surprised when she began pulling him in towards her. He was most surprised when he pulled himself away.

"Yes, I'm listening. I'm sorry, Caitlin, I didn't mean it like that. I suppose that even I get jealous."

Instead of trying to understand any of it, he just embraced her and whispered, once again, "You have the prettiest heartbeat."

After all, he was only human.

ROOF SITTING

Peter sat out in the sun on his own roof. It was past midday, so the world was cooling down. Still, the sun shone bright enough to redden his skin.

The shorts that Peter had on were bunched up around his waist. He wanted to tan as much of his body as possible. He was wearing no shirt.

His parents had just told him that they were getting divorced.

In one of his hands was *Burning in Water and Drowning in Flame*, one of Bukowski's poetry collections. Peter liked to read this kind of stuff while overlooking the endless rows of white, carbon copied houses.

In his other hand was a pen from a resort up north that his parents had taken him to when he was younger. He would underline or circle or star things in the book that he liked.

Peter caught Joyce out of the corner of his eye. It almost looked like she was exiting from his house below. If she saw him, she did nothing to let him know.

This made Peter think about Caitlin. Why did Dylan get her? Why not him?

When Peter got distracted from the book that he was reading, the pen in his right hand would drift to his leg, start drawing the outlines of women. Sketches with emphasis on the breasts, on the hips. Sometimes, he would have the hair cover the nipples.

He looked at his toned thighs, the two inside facing surfaces that only ever saw each other. He thought about his friends who he had known to slash their bodies open in this space. Peter thought that it made sense; if you were to do it anywhere, and you truly wanted it hidden, there was no better place to do it than on your thighs.

He had tried once himself, but he couldn't quite bring himself to do it. His goal had been to feel what his friends had described, a curiosity thing, really. What about it made it feel like a release? He had not found the answer that he was looking for.

Peter thought back to a time in his school's newspaper class when he saw cut marks on the inside of a girl's arm. It was a big school, so he didn't know the girl. But instead of pointing it out to his classmates sitting on either side of him, he brought it to the manager's attention. He told Peter to cover the wounds with a photo editing app.

Because of this, Peter was oddly satisfied with himself. He was happy that he did not let everyone around him know.

At the time, he had felt like a good person.

He looked at the pen marks on his thighs. He would start with the breasts each time. If he messed up, he would try again on a different part of his thigh. It looked like there were many imperfect lower-case w's on his legs, rounded letters, perhaps scars in their own right.

But these scars would wash away.

When he had started drawing, Peter had set down the book that he was holding in his left hand. Now free, he felt the warm shingles that he was sitting on. Sensation exploded in his hand as he moved it across the rough grain of his roof. Peter looked up at the sun. Joyce was no longer anywhere to be seen.

DOUBT

"Do you just like me because I'm young?" Joyce asked Alastair. They were both naked in his bed.

"It's always more than that," he said. The more that he was talking about was her body.

"Like what?"

"You remind me of myself when I was young."

"So, it is because I'm young." She grabbed her phone and started browsing through it.

Alastair's wife had left a few nights ago, after he told her that they were getting a divorce. She had returned briefly to help break the news to Peter but left again immediately afterwards.

"No. It's because you're like me." This, at least, was partly true. Alastair did feel that Joyce was as inwardly cold as he was. But he did not think that she knew this, and it did not make him like her.

"How so?"

"You want something more." Alastair also thought that this was true. But he believed that, unlike him, she was not actively looking for that something more. She was like everyone else.

Wanting without chasing.

She set her phone back down and rested her hands on his chest. She laid her head against it, too. He was on his back, staring straight up at the ceiling.

Earlier, Alastair glimpsed some street light that slid in through his window. It made a column of light. At the moment, he thought that maybe he should try to appreciate it. He did not feel that he had time to.

No time to appreciate a ray of light?

"Do you ever cry, Alastair?"

"No, I have nothing to cry about."

"I think that you will."

"When? When you break my heart?" he joked.

[55]

"I don't think you have a heart to break." In his head, Alastair agreed. Joyce continued, "When you're supposed to shed a tear, you will."

Part of Alastair wondered if there was wisdom in that statement. The other part of Alastair was hoping that his body froze in place and a shadow man appeared to kill both him and Joyce.

THE LAST WARLORD

Roy was dreaming about a horse race occurring in open nature. The course was in a vast, rocky area, with fields and trees and turns interrupting the otherwise desolate waste.

Roy was viewing the whole thing from above, watching each of the jockeys charge across the course, small bodies low and close to their horses. Each had a frightening speed, it seemed as if they were one with their mounts.

One of the racers was not like the others. Rather than being a modern man, he appeared to be a warlord who would have roamed the steppes of old, ages ago. He was tall, proud, riding his horse with an upright back. He was adorned in the most miraculous jewel encrusted armor. He had a necklace bearing the charm of a purple moon.

The man was a sight that would invoke both fear and awe, like a god of war.

Roy could tell that something was off. This sort of race, it could not be meant for this warlord, it was not his home. He was meant to rove and raid, not run and test his speed against others. Roy knew that even though the other racers were lighter loads and would beat the warlord, none of them would be able to outrun this man's bow.

Then, as he was taking a very tight corner, the warlord spilled off of his mount. Roy approached him, asked him why he was even participating to begin with.

"There is no other place for me," the Warlord responded.

Roy considered. "Someone of your skill doesn't just fall off of a horse like that," he noted.

"If I am forced to compete in a race not meant for me, I would rather crash and burn in a notable way than be silently forgotten as I finish last."

Roy understood.

THINGS SAID IN THE NIGHT

"Where were you tonight, Joyce?" asked Grace. Grace was sitting in the family's den and called to Joyce as she was walking over towards the stairs after having just come in.

It was 2:51 a.m.

"I was out."

"Where can you walk home from at nearly 3 in the morning?"

"Do you think because dad's too weak to be a prick, you have to make up for?"

"Dad fought with Mom tonight. He's convinced that she's cheating on him," said Grace. She was biting her nails.

"It took him long enough to figure it out."

"Don't act like you knew."

"Don't act like it's hard to see. Dad's pathetic, he lets her walk all over him."

"Glad to see you care about him."

"You're so fucking dramatic, ever since that trolley thing. Everything always has to be so serious now."

Grace had been sitting the whole time. Finally, she stood up and walked towards her sister.

"That's the first time I've heard you mention it. Why can none of you acknowledge it? I tried forgetting it, and I did. For a while. But it's still there. Shit like that doesn't just go away. I need to talk about it, to understand it. You're too fucking busy staring at your goddamn phone to notice it, to notice that I'm in pain, Joyce! Don't you care about me? Don't you care about anyone?" Grace smelt the alcohol on Joyce's breath. Joyce was quiet, just breathing through her mouth.

"It's always about you, Grace. Never me. Dad thinks Alastair is divorcing his wife because he's fucking our mom. But guess what? I'm fucking Alastair, Grace. Not Mom. Though I'm sure she's off fucking someone else."

With that, Joyce went to bed. Grace continued to stand in the family den, biting her nails.

Alone.

[58]

THE BEGINNING OF SOMETHING

Grace swiped through guys on a dating app. She set her age range to the maximum.

Paul. This guy looked well put together. What did you know, it was a match.

She messaged him, "Hi :)."

In an hour or so, he responded. He was back in town for a couple days, visiting some college friends. He had actually graduated from the same college that Grace was going to now, wasn't that funny?

Yeah, it'd be awesome if they could hang out while he was here. Grace would love that.

They scheduled their get-together at the same time as that block party. Grace didn't want to be there anyway.

Part of her hoped that maybe she would get to watch the moon turn purple with Paul.

BURIED ALIVE

Roy was trying to sleep, but he couldn't stop thinking about his fear of dying in an age that wouldn't remember him. The blankets he lay under felt like the weight of the endless flow of information bearing down on him, burying him inside of himself. It was like a straight jacket of another's design.

Paralyzed. The only thing he could do to crawl out of his grave would be to open his phone, be reassured that people still wanted to hear from him, that he was still needed. Then, he could set it down and go to sleep.

No, the uncertainty and discomfort would immediately return.

Buried alive.

Instead of looking at the piece of plastic and wires resting by him, he ripped his sheets off and rolled out of bed. The first thing that he noticed was the way the street light slid in through the window. It made a column that landed on the floor.

The day that the moon turned purple. That would be a good day for something big to happen.

THERADY

"Does it matter how bad you are on the inside if you do good things?" Alastair asked his therapist.

"Helping people matters. But if you have something on the inside causing you discomfort, something that you know shouldn't be there, you need to get it out in the open. That way, we can see what it is. We can see where it came from and why it's hanging around and bothering you."

"I've always been like this on the inside."

"Can you try thinking back to the first time that you had a thought that you didn't like? The first time that you can remember one in particular?"

There was silence. This was only Alastair's third appointment, but he felt comfortable enough with the woman to be honest, even though part of him despised her for having any power over him.

It doesn't matter what I say here, thought Alastair. She can't tell anyone. I can find another therapist if she hates me for this. So, he ended the silence with a story.

"One day, when I was 14, I thought about doing a bad thing to my grandfather. He was a good man; he didn't do anything bad to me. He cared for me when I needed him. He cared for me, and he loved me. And I thought about killing him.

"He had a closet with books in it, sort of like a hall with one door. He went in to grab a book that he thought I should read. I followed.

"He was very well read, a professor before retirement. And he had his back to me. I saw that it would be difficult for him to turn around in the tight hall.

"I noticed that one of his favorite books was eye level with me. *The Stranger*, by Albert Camus. It was a hardcover edition. I hadn't read it yet, but he had told me about it a million times. Have you ever read it?"

"No, I haven't," the therapist responded. She had a look on her face that invited elaboration.

"Well, it's about one man killing another, seemingly at random. After the murder, the man spends the rest of the book waiting for his own execution in a prison cell."

The therapist nodded, and Alastair continued.

"My grandfather was kneeling now, still with his back to me. He was a bit taller than me, but, in the moment, I was above him.

"I wondered what would happen if I took his favorite book from the shelf and hit him with it in the back of the head, very hard. As hard as I could. I pictured him falling forward a bit, a little staggered."

The therapist was hiding any emotion from her face.

"I imagined him turning as much as he could to look back at me, confused, hurt. Why would I do this to him?"

Alastair's eyes were not watering. He wanted them to be.

"The entire time that I was thinking about it, I felt so unusual, if that word works, if it makes sense. I wanted to be upset, but I couldn't. I just pictured myself hitting him again, and again, and again, until I didn't have to hit him anymore, until the expression on his face was as lifeless as I felt that I was."

The therapist was trying not to wince; she was trying her best to look calm, composed, thoughtful, slightly nodding every few moments as if she were pretending to analyze an opera or a play. Alastair saw through to her fear, but he continued anyways.

"While I was thinking these awful, terrible things about my grandfather, he was looking for a book that he loved so that he could share it with me. And all I could do was picture myself lying down on the floor with him, embracing his corpse. I was hoping that maybe that image would move my soul, maybe that would create some sense of guilt, or regret, or anything. Why didn't that picture of myself lying with my grandfather's corpse, lifeless in my own hands, why didn't it make me feel bad? Why didn't it make me feel evil?"

Alastair's brow was twitching as he was concentrating with intensity, fighting through the pain of remembering.

"Well, what did you feel?" asked the therapist.

"I felt something. I felt guilt. But it was only guilt for the fact that I did not feel guilt, that I could even create such a ghastly image, let alone live with it.

"I was more concerned with the fact that I was not normal than I was with the fact that I pictured a man I loved, a man I admired, violently murdered. By me.

"A normal person would feel guilt for hitting a pedestrian in the street. I would feel guilty about having to pretend that I felt guilt. I cannot be who I am. It's not allowed.

"I lie to everyone. I make them think I am like them. Because I can't let them know that I am not."

Pain was contorting Alastair's face. Still, there were no tears.

The therapist continued to nod.

There was a bit of sunlight that dimly fought through a closed shade between Alastair and the therapist. He hated the weak column of light that landed at his feet.

MECHANICAL DEATH

Dylan fell asleep and found his way to the bottom of the ocean.

There, he saw a tunnel bore into the edifice of a rocket. A small fish swims in front of it. Silently and elegantly, a large, worm like creature smoothly glides out of its cavernous home, mouth gaping. The fish is swallowed, terrified for perhaps a fraction of a second before the toothless, vacuum-like mouth of the serpent closes around it. The serpent recedes back into its lair.

Just like that, the fish is gone.

The event continues to replay in Dylan's head. He thought that it was a strange, sleek, mechanical death, the serpent jutting gracefully in and out, in and out.

All he could think was that with the vastness of the sea, that fish just had to be in front of that hole at that time.

VOLUME III: UNDER A VIOLET SKY

ENVY

It was 2 p.m. on a Sunday, and half of the housing development was drunk. The place was a sprawling complex, containing something like 100 units. There was a block party around the start of summer of each year, but this time it was moved up a little bit into the spring, on the day the moon would turn purple. The party would taper off around 5 p.m. as everyone left to do their own thing before the moon shifted. The festivities had started at 10 a.m., so it was a long day for most.

Peter walked by Caitlin a number of times without being acknowledged by her. Peter knew that she saw him, just as he saw her. Dylan was there, too.

In a moment, Peter would walk up to the two and say hi. After initiating contact, he would be accepted with open arms. That was the kind of party it was--even when lubricated with alcohol, everyone in the neighborhood was stiff until they were sure the social interaction would be a success. They felt like they were being watched too closely to chance the casual nod or smile of recognition; what might happen if the person they waved at ignored them and someone else caught the failure? It was a truly stressful and high stakes event.

"Oh, hey Peter! I didn't know you were out today!" Caitlin said in the bubbly way that a friendly girl who has had a few drinks tends towards when she sees a familiar face.

Peter hugged Caitlin. "How are you doing?" he asked.

"Great, yourself?" asked Caitlin.

"Fucking hammered," he said. It was true, too. It was also the kind of party in which the parents would turn a blind eye to the alcohol consumption of minors, not that they usually wouldn't; on a day like today, however, they were just more open about it.

Caitlin laughed. Peter finally acknowledged Dylan, saying, "What's up, bro?"

The two embraced in the way that guys who are friends do.

"Not much, man. You?"

[67]

"Just living life. How have you two been?"

The expression on Dylan's face showed that he knew how loaded that question might be.

Caitlin smiled with both embarrassment and compassion, saying, "Good, Peter. We've been good."

At this, Peter decided that it was time to move on to the next group.

After stumbling through the crowd, occasionally taking the bold step to say hi to the people that he knew, but always avoiding eye contact with the people who he only half knew, Peter ended up finding his father. He was talking to Joyce and her mother.

"You really do have a lovely daughter, Melissa," complimented Alastair.

"She raised herself," replied Joyce's mother.

I did, too, thought Peter. "Hey, Dad," he said.

"Hey, Peter, I'm sure that you've met Joyce before, right? I think you two might hit it off," said Alastair. Peter knew how much these hollow, copy and paste phrases killed his father. He was probably only here ironically, or to get laid.

"We went to high school together for a little, actually," Peter said. "I think you were a senior when I was a freshman?" He was paying attention to Joyce, now, as the pair began talking. More of the mindless, how's it been, where do you go now, haha you're drunk? I'm drunk, too. The moon will look so pretty tonight.

At the same time, Melissa and Alastair kept chatting.

"I have to acknowledge the elephant in the room, I just do: you're getting a divorce?" Melissa asked Alastair. He was not taken aback by the question.

"It feels like it's for the best. I can't keep going on like this, I feel like I'm taking advantage of her. She is so much more of a passionate person than I am. I'm robbing her of the intensity she deserves."

"Trust me, no woman that you ever spent time with could feel that she was being taken advantage of. She'd just be lucky to be in your company."

This was normally acceptable--Alastair's confident but casual posture and disinterested look often invited these kinds of comments, even when he was not fishing for them. However, Francis was approaching and caught the tail end of his wife's statement.

Alastair said hi. Melissa did not.

"What are we talking about?"

Peter and Joyce were now paying more attention to the adults' words than their own.

"Oh, just how Alastair is going to be free soon," said Melissa.

"Thanks to you, Francis. I really appreciated the talk the other night."

"Anything for a *friend*." Emphasis was on the word friend.

"Have you seen Grace, dad?" Joyce asked as Peter was in the middle of a sentence that even he was not paying attention to. She rarely ever used the word dad.

"No, I haven't. She's your sister and your daughter, you'd think one of you would know where she is," Francis said as he motioned to Joyce and Melissa in kind.

"She's just as much your daughter as she is mine," said Melissa. Alastair was uncomfortable now. He looked at Peter.

"Oh, I know, but I don't think that you do. I'm the only one who acts like we're related. I thought you two may have forgotten that we're a fucking family."

"Sorry to have to run, but I'm going to go grab another drink. Peter, do you want to walk with me?" inquired Alastair.

As Peter began to speak, Francis said, "You know, Alastair, I think that you might be part of this family, too, in one way or another. Now that you're so free," he said while shaking his own hands back and forth, "you can spend more time with my wife and me, or maybe just my wife, if you'd like that better. I really did enjoy that conversation we had the other night."

"I don't know what kind of idea you've got going, but I assure you, it's way off," Alastair stated. The words had a sharp edge.

Heads from other groups were beginning to turn now.

"Dad, I think you've had a little too much," Joyce said.

"I can handle my liquor, Joyce."

Embarrassed, Melissa grabbed Francis' arm and said, "Well, at least come and grab a snack with me. I hear the Millers are grilling up burgers."

"And I really do need that drink now. But it was good to see you all. Francis, Melissa, Joyce. Come on, Peter," Alastair stated as he smiled smuggly and waved at each of them in turn. The smile that Joyce returned was the most inviting.

[69]

"Don't drink too much, Alastair. You might make a decision that you can't undo," warned Francis.

With that, the two families separated.

TOO CLOSE

At their lunch, Grace became impressed at the amount of money that Paul had. A few years of consulting, and he was already driving around in a new convertible. Leased, of course; he said he hated the idea of saving money until he died. He would rather spend it on monthly car payments than let it go to the kids he would never have.

Paul was slim, too. Almost unnaturally slim. Grace thought that this added to the mystique that the businessman had carefully cultivated.

"You remind me of someone," he told her.

"And who might that be? One of your past lovers?" Grace was trying to say what she thought Joyce might say.

"Something like that. More of an old friend."

Grace caught herself biting her nails.

The two had ended up in Paul's hotel room during the middle of the day. This was the first time Grace had gotten this comfortable this quickly with any guy. It was some combination of his charm and her loneliness.

The two were partially clothed and making out. Grace asked, "Can I tell you something that I did?"

Paul sensed the serious tone in her voice and matched it, "What do you mean, something that you did?"

Grace was laying on her back now, looking up at the ceiling.

"Something that I'm not proud of, but other people don't seem to care about. Almost like they think it's okay that I did it."

"We all do things that we aren't proud of," Paul said. He was sitting up, leaning over Grace. One of his hands was playing with her hair.

"I killed someone."

Paul did not know how to respond, so he laid down next to her. He rolled her over to her side, so that she was facing him. He pulled her head to the skin over his chest that was as tight as a drum. He held her there.

Grace kept talking, explaining everything.

When she was done, Paul said, "I would have done the same thing, I think."

"Really?"

"What else was there for you to do? Let five people die? Sometimes, you have to give up a little so that you can save a lot."

"What have you given up, Paul?"

"Temporary happiness. I keep sacrificing it, every day. I don't let anyone get too close, because I know that the one I'm waiting for will be more than worth it."

Grace pulled her head away from his chest so that her eyes could meet his.

"No, that sounds like you're killing a lot of people for one. That's the opposite of what I did."

"Not if this one person is worth five times everyone else combined," Paul smiled at her. It was the inviting kind of smile, the warm one that said that everything would be more than alright. Grace misinterpreted this smile and the conversation.

"What's her name?" she asked in a whisper.

"Christine."

When Grace thought that the block party would finally be over, she had Paul take her home.

THE VERGE OF

After a weak attempt at sobering up, Francis left the party early to drive to the beach in his hometown.

He had settled down about an hour away from the place that he was born. He had first gone to the place that he now lived in for its college. He had stayed because he had met Melissa.

He had lost his virginity to her. Then, he married her.

And now, he was certain that she was fucking Alastair.

Out of his car, Francis felt the sand beneath his feet, somehow a solid, somehow a liquid. Like grain.

He had really always liked Alastair. Alastair was admirable, in a strange way. Very reserved, stoic almost. Except for the other night that Francis had spoken with him about Alastair's own wife, the man almost never revealed what he was thinking.

On the other hand, Francis quite often did. His daughters hated him for it, he knew. Maybe his wife did, too.

The moon would be purple tonight.

As much as Francis admired Alastair, part of him had to hate him. The man was sitting there telling Francis about how he felt like he was being dishonest to his own wife--what about to Francis? Who had the audacity to lie to his friends face?

Maybe Francis liked that about Alastair, too. His audacity. Not many people had the balls to fuck your wife and then get drinks with you to talk about divorce.

Alastair had done a lot in his time. There was so much that Francis still wanted to do himself before he died. Maybe this would be his chance.

Grace and Joyce were both in college. They didn't need him anymore, they never did. Francis could just divorce Melissa and get on with everything else he wanted to do.

Her. His wife. He always referred to her as "his wife" or "her," even when he was just thinking to himself. He rarely ever thought about "her" as Melissa.

It was creeping towards evening. Francis sat down in the sand, so that his feet were in the water. The waves were gently lapping. In the brief moments of recession, when the high water mark on his legs was exposed, the cool lake breeze stung the wet spots in a refreshing way. It made Francis feel more alive.

He had to do something. He had always wanted to learn how to sail. Perhaps he would buy a boat and travel the world. All by himself. Why not? That's what Alastair had said that he would do.

Francis pretended that the water in front of him was the ocean. He pictured a large, expensive boat sitting out there. All his.

If he divorced his wife and left his children on their own, who would sail with him?

Francis couldn't think of any friends who would be willing to drop everything and leave their lives like that.

Alastair would do that, though. Buy a boat and disappear. He said he would.

Francis's hand became a white knuckled fist as he reminded himself that Alastair was most definitely fucking his wife.

Still a little drunk, he got back in his car and headed towards home.

WINTER NIGHTMARES

Peter was in his bedroom. He was sitting at his desk in front of the large window. If he opened it and walked out and turned to the left, he could go up and behind his room; it offered a lot of space to read or write or tan or drink or simply sit.

Sometimes, the light of the moon landed so that he could see his roof glowing under its pale light white. Tonight, under the light of the purple moon, there was the shadow of a man in that patch of now violet light.

Peter was shocked. But he was also young and restless. And, since both of his parents were gone, somewhere, he had been drinking their liquor. So, he was not afraid.

He grabbed the hunting knife his father had given him and opened the window.

He got out on the roof and walked around to see who was there. It looked like it was himself, standing on the roof.

"Hello?" Peter asked.

"Don't worry, it's just me. And by me, I mean you."

"Why am I seeing myself?"

"You're the only person that you ever talk to."

"Why is that?"

"Because no one likes us."

"Why not?"

"We're weird."

"Plenty of people are weird."

"But we make them uncomfortable."

Peter looked at the knife in his hand.

"I don't mean to."

"That doesn't change the fact that you do it."

"How can I make them like me?"

"Be yourself."

"I am myself."

"No, you're trying to be your father."

He pressed down and ran the blade against his right palm. A little bit of blood was drawn.

"What's wrong with that? Isn't everybody their Dad in a way?"

"In a way. But less so when he's fucking one of the girls they have a crush on."

"Why does he do that?"

"Because he's lonely. And because he can."

Peter gently smeared the blood against his wrist.

"I'm lonely, too, but I can't get with her. Won't being like him make it so I can do what he can do?"

"Do you want to do what he does?"

"It seems to work for him."

"Does it, though?"

Peter paused and let the strange light from the purple moon shine off of the blade.

"I don't know."

"You know that he isn't any happier than you are."

"How can I be sure?"

"Because he's leaving a woman who never did anything wrong to him, he's leaving someone who still loves him more than anything. Just because he is bored."

"I'm bored."

With that, Peter brought the knife up to his neck. He lightly tapped the blade against his flesh and prepared to sharply press in and drag it to the right.

"Give that to me." Other Peter beckoned to the knife.

"Why?"

"There is enough death tonight."

Peter did as he was told. Other Peter threw the knife off the roof and disappeared. Peter sat down beneath the purple moon.

A police car pulled into his driveway.

SITTING ON A TOMBSTONE

Roy was sitting on top of the bell tower on his campus. The one with the circle of grass around it. And a fountain by it. The once inscribed with somebody's dead last name.

Above him, the sky was dimming.

Funny how his plan would line up so nicely with the asteroid streaking through the air. Almost like someone had planned it out.

Roy knew that people did that, they just planned things around phenomenon; that way, it felt like they were the ones in charge of the random event. That way, it happened for them. There was that party on campus that he had seen a sign for, for instance. The one hosted by the school. The one that no one would attend.

Roy didn't like planning things that relied on other people going out of their way to make it work. So, he had made his plan one that only worked if people were doing what they were always doing: ignoring beauty.

As the rock flew by hundreds of miles above him, he would flip the switch that he held in his hand. It would disrupt all wifi in the area and cut off access to cellular reception while unilaterally shutting off all nearby phones.

He knew that the thing in his hand was of impressive design, but he had no one to share it with.

Roy grabbed his own cell phone from his pocket. He thought it would be funny if he put a picture of the contraption online before he used it.

On Instagram, he posted an image with the caption, "What's this?" He knew that no one would hit the like button, even if they could.

It was nearly dark now. His legs were dangling over the edge of the tower. He dropped his cellphone towards the ground, about 100 feet below.

He did not watch it fall. Instead, he looked up at the sky and saw a purple scar appear across the otherwise peaceful canvas.

Roy flipped the switch. After it activated, he dropped the device, too.

He didn't want to keep holding onto something that made him feel like a god.

After all, he was only human.

BY THE LIGHT OF A PHONE

Dylan was on a walk around town. It was growing towards dusk on the night that everyone was supposed to watch the moon turn purple.

Something else was on his mind. He was thinking about Maria. She had just returned to Spain.

Back when she had first rejected him, he had promised her that he would kiss her before she left. "A lot can change in eight months," he had said.

Indeed, a lot had changed, but not the way that he had wanted. He had gotten Caitlin pregnant. She was to have a child. His child.

He had lost his virginity to her, and now they were attached to one another by the bond of a living creature. An abortion was ruled out; he had suggested one in silent hope. She said no.

Still, she had been drinking today. Maybe she was not convinced.

The pair was just now finishing up as seniors in high school--how were they supposed to raise a kid? Would they live with one of their parents? Would they still go to college? Would they both bounce from hourly job to hourly job, devoid of any aspirations except keeping their kid alive?

He wore a condom; she took a pill. Where had he, where had they gone wrong? Were they really just that unlucky? Were they really just the fraction of the percent of the fraction of the percent this had happened to? Life seemed so random.

Dylan resigned to pulling out his phone, opening it to his home page, swiped to the right. He clicked on Instagram, scrolled three pictures down his discovery feed. Then, he opened his direct messages, saw one from Maria and one from Caitlin. He opened the one from Maria.

It was a meme about missing someone. How niche and timely. He was sure she had gone looking for it. He hearted the message and closed the app.

Dylan clicked on the box that he kept all of his messaging apps in and started with Snapchat. He scrolled through the 32 snaps that he had not yet opened, responded to five of them. His selection felt random, but Dylan knew that it was the five people he most wanted approval from. Dylan swiped over to the stories side of the app, looked at seven or so, following the same logic. Then, he darted back over to the private snaps, opened the two that he had gotten back from the five that he had sent and quickly responded.

He opened his messenger app, looked at the six messages. Two of them, from his parents, he had been ignoring. Three of them were friends he would respond to one was from Maria. He clicked on her name, read the message that said, "I miss you :(." He closed the app without responding to any of them.

He opened Tinder. He was still dating Caitlin, but he liked to look. After swiping through four girls, he already felt bad. He was going to be a father to a child with Caitlin.

He closed the app and went back to Instagram. He opened the discovery section, scrolled through memes for four minutes, sending two to Caitlin, one to a friend, Brian.

Dylan switched back over to messages, answered the three he had ignored, one of which was actually from Brian. Brian was inviting him to drink with him tonight.

Dylan closed his messages and started heading back to Snapchat.

Then, a message from Maria. He let the notification banner disappear.

Slowly, he made his way back over to messages. He saw it's preview: "I love you."

At that, his phone went black. Dylan stopped walking. Did it run out of battery or something? He tried turning it back on. Had that message that he saw even been real?

Then, Dylan heard a violent swerve and felt himself pushed from behind, hard. He stumbled forwards, twisted around so that he landed on his ass and saw a car where he had just been standing, plowing ahead with an older man rolling over its roof.

It was a strange, sleek, mechanical death, the car jutting elegantly out into the crosswalk. Even though it drove on, Dylan pictured it backing up.

In, out. In, out.

Dylan noticed that the corpse of the man who had saved him was strangely purple. Everything was purple.

He looked up. He had missed the asteroid.

The sky was now violet.

ALONE?

Grace was sitting alone in her room.

Above her and outside, the sky was dimming.

Grace had grown accustomed to the dark, though. It felt like she was always living in it. She had tried to bury the source of her guilt but could not.

In front of her, there was a big window that let her walk out onto her roof, if she wanted to. Sometimes, she and Joyce would just lay out there and tan. It seemed that Joyce liked doing that less and less with Grace.

Could Grace ever feel the kind of love that Paul had for Christine?

What if the boy she had killed with the trolley was supposed to be her soulmate? Maybe that would be a weird kind of justice. Painful, she thought, but fair, as all justice should be.

In her left hand, she had a bottle of Vicodin. Her mother had found a reason to receive a prescription and took the pills frequently. Grace had always figured that it had to be an attempt to zone out and ignore her husband. Between that and always being gone, Melissa never really had to deal with Francis.

Grace wished that she would have talked to her Dad more. She had told him that she might be able to watch the sky with him tonight. They used to do that when she was younger, even when nothing special was going on. Them being together made it special enough.

But right now, Grace didn't know where Francis was. And her mother, she was never there. Then her sister was always drunk, or over with Alastair.

Grace hated block parties. She was glad that she had missed the one today. All the conversations felt so superficial.

The purple light slid through the window in front of her. It made an otherworldly column that covered her and the pill bottle in her hand.

Tonight was the night, wasn't it? Grace felt that there would be something weirdly peaceful about going out like this, with the moon as strange as it was.

At peace. Grace thought that was the best way to describe her state of mind right now. At peace, and she had not even taken any of the pills yet. She was not biting her nails. But she was thinking about the most significant time that she had done that.

"You killed my son, and you have to live with that."

No, she didn't.

Slowly, she undid the white cap of the standard orange medicine bottle in her standard house. She poured 20 pills into her hand. The acetaminophen would kill her if she took about 15, but she wanted to be safe; when you got closer to 20, the hydrocodone became lethal, too.

This was not a cry for help.

Grace had tried crying for help. And no one listened to her.

She set down the pill bottle and picked up the large glass of water she had left sitting at her feet. Three or four pills per gulp, she figured. If she choked on them, oh well. No one would be here to hear her gasping for air. Not that she would want air.

She stared at the pills in her hand. She wasn't really looking at them; she was looking at the shimmering purple light that painted the pile. It was quite beautiful.

After swallowing the pills, she laid down on her back and let the purple light coming in through the window color her.

Grace had decided not to leave a note, except for a brief apology to the mother of the boy.

The one she had rehearsed.

Soon, Grace was quiet under a violet sky.

REDEMPTION

Tonight was the night that the moon was supposed to turn purple. Alastair thought that tonight could be the night that he put his foot down with himself, the night that he would change.

He found himself aimlessly wandering through the streets of his town after having left the block party near its end; it was already getting to be evening, so the roads were relatively empty. Nobody was out and about. Alastair wondered if they were waiting somewhere special to watch the moon, or if they had just forgotten about it altogether.

Alastair didn't really care where he would be when it happened, he would just be excited to see the dramatic shift. If even something as ancient as the moon could change like this, if even just for a moment, then Alastair was certain that he could make it pass himself, that he could find the peace that he was looking for.

He was free already, wasn't he? Didn't that imply peace? Was the space that he had earned by alienating his son and wife not enough to win him the serenity that he so desired?

He was fucking a child. She was 21, but he was fucking a child.

They all were children to him.

And this one was his friend's daughter. And all that he could tell his therapist was that he had thought about killing his grandfather when he was 14, not that that was any good.

The difference, though, was that killing his grandfather had been a thought. This was an action.

Was thought inaction? The most inactive that Alastair felt was when he was doing what others would consider to be relaxing or meaningful. Even when he would find himself frozen in his bed, paralyzed by the fear that a dream brought, he felt more active than he did when watching television with his family.

Did Francis really not know that Alastair was having sex with Joyce? Did he really think that it was Melissa? Either way, Alastair knew that he was ruining the friendship.

On purpose?

Up a bit and on the other side of the street, Alastair saw a bar with outdoor seating. It looked like just about everyone there was on their cellphones, sitting and texting.

Above him, the sky was dimming.

Alastair continued forwards, walking by the door of a storefront that was ever so slightly ajar. Most people left their doors closed. Alastair almost went in out of curiosity, but he continued ahead.

An open door?

In front of him, there was a boy walking, texting furiously on his phone. Alastair thought that he recognized him, maybe one of Peter's friends?

What was Peter doing right now?

Alastair thought back to his own parents. His earliest gripe with them had been the closing of his bedroom door. Alastair figured that Peter had plenty more reasons to hate him than that.

How could Alastair dig himself out of this hole?

The boy was crossing the street ahead of Alastair. He was turning left towards the bar. Alastair recognized the name of the place as one that Joyce frequented. Maybe he would stop in for a drink. He prepared to turn here, too.

The crosswalk light had gone red. The boy had stopped walking in the middle of the street. He was looking at his phone. Alastair decided to walk over to him so that he could tell him to keep going. He didn't see a car on either side of him.

As he approached the boy, Alastair caught a vehicle violently turning at the intersection they were standing in. Alastair and the boy would both be hit.

Without thinking, Alastair lunged like a man made of shadows and pushed the boy forwards, away from the car.

Alastair felt the force of more than a ton of steel and rubber and plastic hit his legs and then swipe them out from under him. His shoulder made contact with the hood, and he rolled up the glass, bouncing on the roof, bouncing on the trunk, bouncing on the cement.

Alastair looked up and saw that the moon was purple.

It had changed.

Finally, Alastair released a tear.

HOMECOMING

Francis was still confused when he was driving home. What was he supposed to do? Could he really leave his wife? He wasn't convinced that he could.

Sail the world. With Alastair?

He was back in town now.

Above him, the sky was dimming.

The purple moon was supposed to happen tonight. Everyone had talked and talked about it until it was no longer interesting. Francis himself barely cared about it. He would not be watching it with anyone he loved.

A stop light. Francis obeyed it. A couple was walking the crosswalk. Francis watched them. They were half his age, and they looked happy.

Green.

Francis passed the same doctor's office that he had gone to countless times before. It was in the kind of building immediately flanked by two others with no room for alleys. Most of the town was like this, walls of buildings.

Walls.

When he had the flu his second year in college, he had gone to that same doctor's office. He had also gone there when he had a particularly violent cough in his mid-20s, and when his wife was pregnant before Francis had turned 30.

On and on and on. Until he was at his current age. He didn't even like to think about that number.

Retirement. Was that the freedom he was looking for?

A red light up ahead. There were two people on a crosswalk; Francis would pass them on his right if he went straight. One was a man, and one was a boy.

The man was Alastair.

Alastair.

The man who was fucking Francis's wife.

The man who would never sail with him.

Francis blew the light to turn right without stopping and swerved towards Alastair. If Francis hit the boy as well, oh well.

As he heard the *thud* that a car makes when it hits a body, and then the second and third and fourth *thuds* that it makes when the body lands on the hood and then bounces on the roof and then off of the trunk, Francis decided that he would keep driving.

He would go home to his daughters. That would be nice.

Grace had said that she might want to spend the night watching the sky with him.

Maybe she was still home.

TEARS IN NO RAIN

Joyce was in the outdoor seating at her favorite bar. She was sitting at a table with some friends, all drinking and using their phones.

Above them, the sky was dimming.

When it was darker out, the friends noticed that their phones had turned black. It looked like everyone else's had, too; they were now all looking around.

There were conversations before, but now there were more. Everyone wanted to know what had happened.

Then, a guy was pointing up towards the sky. Heads followed his hands to see what it was about. The sight was really quite gorgeous. Haunting, almost.

Tonight was the night that the moon turned purple.

Joyce still had her drink in her hand. She instinctively went to check her phone. She quickly remembered that it would not work.

Was Grace watching any of this, wondered Joyce? And what about Alastair? She thought it would be romantic if she maybe spent the night with him. She knew that he would find that dumb, though.

Joyce heard a violent swerving and looked over to the street. An older man was rolling over the top of a car, as a boy was on the ground, watching it. The car drove on. Fast.

Was that her father's car?

Everyone at the bar quickly rushed over to the body and the boy, including Joyce. Everyone was asking each other who it was, what had happened? Was the boy okay? The man? Where was the driver?

Joyce saw that the boy was Dylan, the high school kid she had talked to at the block party. She knelt down next to him and helped him up.

"Joyce?"

"You okay? What the hell happened?"

"I was-, I was on my phone, and I guess a car was going to hit me or something. Before it could, that guy over there pushed me out of the way. Is he… is he okay?"

They both pushed forward to see.

When Joyce saw the body, she recognized Alastair.

She knelt down and cradled his head in her lap. She was starting to cry as only the lover of a dead person could.

Joyce saw that there were tears on his cheeks, too, and not just the ones flowing from her face.

Alastair had told her that he didn't cry. Joyce had always said that he could, he just had to be in the right situation.

"When you're supposed to shed a tear, you will."

Joyce couldn't tell him that she had been right all along, because Alastair was dead by the time that she got to him.

EPILOGUE: ROY'S TRIAL

A RACE NOT MEANT FOR HIM

"In closing, it is important for the jury to remember that the defendant committed his crime out of the utmost spite and contempt for his helpless victims. He is a DEFILER of our otherwise functioning society, a cog that is not only broken, but one that *wants* to be broken. Moreover, he harbors the wicked desire that we all break with him."

As the prosecution sat down, the defense attorney began to stand up in that slow, smooth way that lawyers are paid to stand, even when they know, beyond a shadow of a doubt, that all hope is lost.

The attorney coolly sauntered to the center of the room, looked first at the judge, then the jury, then the audience and cameras. It felt more like a TV special than a trial.

"Your honor, this is about the time I would break off into a steamy, impassioned speech in hopes of giving my client one last chance at freedom. However, I have received a request from my client, the kind of request that I often receive from a client: a request to close on his own behalf.

"Usually, I would deter any client of mine from proceeding in such a reckless endeavor; this individual, however, has a level of eloquence and poise not usually possessed by the typical defendant of mine. This fact has provoked me to actually promote, rather than deter, his speaking.

"I think it is important that you all remember who it is that you are trying today. Not a typical man, no, not at all. No, no." A playful but serious finger wag here with a pause for emphasis: "You are trying a man with belief."

The defense attorney sat down in the same cool way that he had first risen.

Roy stood up, imitating the patterns he had seen from the lawyer as much as possible. Roy was abnormally capable of elegant movements across the room. Something about his silver hair, shining against the flash of the countless cameras, made these motions seem all the more powerful, like he was some sort of prince of old descending from his palace to address the masses. Even though he was being tried, perhaps he felt this other idea to be more accurate.

Roy looked around the big courthouse. It was old, perhaps one of the oldest buildings in the city. The walls still had their original dark wood paneling. There were tall windows spaced every five feet or so on either side down the length of the room. The wooden benches were filled with people. This seemed like as good a place as any for the event.

Roy cleared his throat and began to speak:

"On the night of my supposed crime, the Head of Mímir passed over our planet and drastically changed our perception of the moon, if only for a moment. The scientists have told us why this was possible. The astronomers explained what this meant for our understanding of the universe. The religious told us what their gods intended on communicating. The philosophers discussed what it meant for humanity. The poets told us why we should find it beautiful. Everyone had something different to say about the same situation. The same can be said about the thing that I did on that day.

"You all can call me a criminal. You can say I destroyed your property, you can argue that I robbed you of the services you paid for, if only for a moment. You can even blame the hit and run that occurred on me, but we have all learned that there was much more to that particular incident than first thought.

"You are all free to view my actions in those contexts, if you feel that you must. Otherwise, you can view it as my attempt at liberating your minds.

"How many of you would not have seen the miracle of the purple moon if I had not interrupted your rampant cell phone usage? How many of you would just have seen videos or pictures of people standing under it who were not even looking at it themselves?

"Every morning, you wake up to the alarm on your cell phone. Every morning, you lay in your bed, scrolling through the different messages you've received on the different apps that populate your device. You allow someone else to tell you what to think before you even have a chance to make that decision for yourself.

"You go to work or school and wait for your break so you can simply pull out your phone and get lost in all the noises and colors. And do you know what you do to pass the time until that break comes? Certainly not work or learn. No, you sit on your cell phone as you wait to sit on your cell phone. It is both the beginning and the end of everything you do.

"You go home, finally able to unwind. You may do a little work while still being sure to check your messages every three minutes. Maybe you grab a beer or pour a glass of wine and put on the mind numbing television that you can't even bring yourself to watch--no, you're too busy watching the smaller screen in front of your hands.

"You let the pacifier that is that comforting brick of plastic and wires coax you to sleep, you let it tell you that yes, other people do care about you, they send you messages still, they haven't forgotten that you exist. Your post from earlier today is still getting likes. You're still alive, you're still real.

"Are you, though? Are you alive by staring at the same thing each day? Sure, there's something new, there's always something new, something happening in your bubble that wasn't before. But is it ever really new? Or is it the same people going on about the same ideas in the same way?

"Something new happened, many nights ago. The moon turned purple. Most of you in this town would have missed it, if it weren't for me. I regret nothing of what I did; my only hope is that the change is permanent. Unfortunately, I somehow don't think that it is.

"You go on, watching this trial, consuming it like comfort food, tuned in to today's drama. Tomorrow, you'll watch tomorrow's drama, and the next day, you'll watch the next day's drama, ad infinitum. You'll listen to predictions of things to come, oh, that's exciting! But you'll never actually notice them happening.

"On your deathbed, do you know what you'll remember? That one time you saw that one cool thing on your cell phone. That one time you laughed at that one joke that someone posted. Christ, I'm sure that half of you already dream about the times that you were on your device.

"The cell phone is the new opium of the masses. You can keep using it to numb the pain, or you can cut yourself off, however difficult it may be.

"You can say I am a thief, that I stole the connectivity that you were paying for. But, tell me, who is the greater thief: myself, or the phone in your pocket?"

The jury found Roy guilty on all charges.

As he was being ushered out of the great big hall, he noticed the way that the sun slid through the large windows on one of the walls. It made a column of light.

He smiled.

Made in the USA
Columbia, SC
18 August 2020